NEWS HOUNDS

THE

LAURA JAMES · Illustrated by CHARLIE ALDER

BLOOMSBURY
CHILDREN'S BOOKS

LONDON   OXFORD   NEW YORK   NEW DELHI   SYDNEY

BLOOMSBURY CHILDREN'S BOOKS
Bloomsbury Publishing Plc
50 Bedford Square, London WC1B 3DP, UK
29 Earlsfort Terrace, Dublin 2, Ireland

BLOOMSBURY, BLOOMSBURY CHILDREN'S BOOKS and the Diana logo
are trademarks of Bloomsbury Publishing Plc

First published in Great Britain in 2021 by Bloomsbury Publishing Plc

A catalogue record for this book is available from the British Library

ISBN: PB: 978-1-5266-2054-5; eBook: 978-1-5266-2055-2

2 4 6 8 10 9 7 5 3 1

Typeset by Tracey Cunnell

Printed and bound in China by C&C Offset Printing Co. Ltd
Shenzhen, Guangdong

MIX
Paper from
responsible sources
FSC® C008047

To find out more about our authors and books visit www.bloomsbury.com
and sign up for our newsletters

For Sienna and William – L.J.

For J&W ... no, you can't have

a dog ... yet – C.A.

Gizmo was a city dog. A prince of the urban jungle. His paths were clear, and his lawns were mown. He and Grannie owned the streets they...

GRANNIE MAKES SURPRISE MOVE
TO THE COUNTRY TO WRITE MEMOIRS!
GIZMO SHOCKED!

Gizmo worried as he and Grannie
drove away from the only home
he'd ever known. They were going
to a place called Puddle. That didn't
sound good – he hated getting his

paws wet. But where Grannie went,
he went.

Gizmo had finally managed to
nap, when a bump in the road woke
him. They'd arrived. He sniffed the
air. It smelt ... different. Too clean.

His worry deepened.

As Grannie made her way to the house, Gizmo explored the garden. It seemed very strange to him. For a start there wasn't a smartly dressed park attendant.

There were no fountains, no rows of benches, and where were the rubbish bins? To him it seemed wild and unruly. He was carefully edging his way around a flower bed when he heard a voice.

'Hello there!'

Was it the great dog in the sky?

'Over here!' said the voice.

Gizmo looked all around but
he couldn't see anyone. Ahead of
him was a white fence with a
small hole in it. He peered through.
More wilderness. All he could see
were shrubs and bushes and four
strange hairy tree trunks.

'Is there anybody there?' he asked.

'Yes, me!' came the reply.

Suddenly his gaze was met by
an enormous eye. He jumped back,
startled, and the eye blinked.

'I'm Jilly,' it said. 'Pleased to
meet you.'

Gizmo tried to wag his tail in a
friendly way, but he was shaking.

'Um, hello,' he replied. 'I'm Gizmo. I've never met an enormous eye before.'

'Up here,' insisted the voice. 'At the top of the fence.'

Gizmo craned his head back as far as he could and saw the biggest, furriest face he'd ever seen. He recognised the eye.

'What are you?' he asked, amazed.

'I'm an Irish wolfhound!'

'What are you standing on?'
Gizmo asked. He couldn't work out
how she could be looking over the
fence when it was so high.

'Nothing,'
said Jilly,
confused.

Gizmo looked back through the hole in the fence and realised that what he'd thought were tree trunks were in fact Jilly's very long legs. She was the biggest dog he'd ever seen! He took a nervous step back.

'What are *you*?' Jilly asked.

'I'm a dachshund,' Gizmo replied. Despite his nerves he couldn't help showing off his long, smooth body. 'Or a sausage dog. It's easier to say.'

'Mmm, sausages!' said Jilly, salivating. A droplet landed on Gizmo's head as Jilly leaned over the fence.

'Don't eat me! Don't eat me!' Gizmo cried, covering his eyes with his paws. 'I'm not a sausage! I'm a sausage DOG!'

Above him, he heard a snuffling, woofing sound. Jilly was laughing. 'I'm not going to eat you!' she said. 'Sorry I drooled. I just love sausages – ever since I had my pups, I'm always hungry.' Eventually her chuckling got the better of Gizmo and he joined in. Maybe he'd made his first friend in Puddle!

From the garden behind Jilly there was a whine. Putting his eye to the hole in the fence,

Gizmo saw a
puppy tugging
on Jilly's tail.

'Meet Wolfie,'
said Jilly, wagging
her tail free. Wolfie
gave a little bark.
'He's my naughty one,' said Jilly
fondly. 'Always wanting attention.
My other three, Wilfred, Wilma
and Willabelle, are in the garden
playing. Or at least I hope they are!'

Even though Wolfie was still a puppy, he was already taller than Gizmo. Gizmo said a shy 'hello', and Wolfie nearly got his nose stuck in the fence in his enthusiastic response. Gizmo had to admit, Wolfie looked very sweet.

'Gizmo! Supper time!'

'That's Grannie. I have to go,' said Gizmo.

'Of course,' said Jilly. 'Come around tomorrow to meet the puppies properly.'

'Gizmooooooo!' Grannie was rattling the kibble tin now.

'I'll see you tomorrow, Jilly!' said Gizmo, before hurrying inside for his food.

The following morning, after
breakfast, Gizmo went to the hole
in the fence and waited for Jilly.
Soon her huge nose was snuffling
at the hole. When she smelt Gizmo,
she heaved a huge, sad sigh.

'Are you OK, Jilly?' Gizmo asked.

'Meet me out the front,' she told him.

Gizmo did as he was told and squeezed through the bars of his garden gate to wait for Jilly. With her were all four of her puppies. They were a charming if rough-and-tumble lot, pulling on each other's ears and tails. Gizmo could tell that Jilly was very proud of them, but that

there was something making her
very sad.

Jilly made the introductions.
'This is Wolfie, who you met last
night.' Wolfie gave a loud bark
and then immediately sat down
to scratch his ear. 'This is Wilfred.'
Wilfred hid behind Jilly. 'He's quite
shy,' Jilly told Gizmo in a whisper.
One of the puppies then stood in
between Jilly's paws. 'Wilma.'

'Hello, Wilma,' said Gizmo.

'And last but not least, Willabelle.' Willabelle rushed towards Gizmo and licked him.

Gizmo flapped his ears in amusement. 'Lovely to meet you all,' he said. 'What a charming family you have, Jilly,' he added.

'They are sweet, aren't they?' she replied as the puppies began to race each other back and forth under the hedge. As soon as they were out of earshot, Jilly burst out, 'Oh, Gizmo, something terrible has happened!'

Gizmo looked at his new friend in concern. 'What, Jilly?'

'My owners are planning to sell the puppies by the end of the week. They're going to be sent

far away from Puddle and I'm
never going to get to see them
again.'

Gizmo put his paw on Jilly's.
'This is terrible news,' he
sympathised. 'What can I do
to help you?'

'I thought we could ask around
the village today and see if any
of the other dogs can help find
homes for the puppies. Will
you come with us? It'll be a

good way for you to meet everyone,'
said Jilly.

'Of course!' said Gizmo.
'Don't worry, Jilly, I'm
sure someone will
be able to help us.'

'Thank you, Gizmo,' replied Jilly. 'You're a true friend.'

Jilly organised the puppies
as best she could, reminding
them to keep their paws clean,

and they set off. It wasn't long
before the puppies were running
ahead.

Gizmo was both excited by and
nervous about the chance to
explore the village and meet
its residents. They'd just passed
the school when something or
someone shot past them like a

rocket. Gizmo was so taken aback
that he fell into a nearby privet
hedge.

'What was that?!' he asked.

'Oh, that's Lola,' replied Jilly.
'She's always on the run.'

Just then Lola came back into view. 'What's up, Jilly?' she asked. 'Oh, and who's your friend?'

'This is Gizmo,' said Jilly, helping Gizmo back on to his feet. 'He's just moved in next door.'

'Gizmo! Lovely to meet you,' Lola said. 'What kind of sports are you into? Stick carrying?'

'No.'

'Chasing squirrels?'

'Um, no, not really.'

'How about pond swimming? There's a lovely one in the middle of the village.'

'I'm not very good at sports,' Gizmo confessed. 'I mostly like napping ... in a chair or on a sofa, sometimes behind the sofa, sometimes in my bed, sometimes even upside down ...' Gizmo trailed off, fondly remembering a particularly good nap he'd had just the other day.

'Wow! You're so versatile,' said
Lola. 'You'll have to teach me how
to sleep upside down one day.

You're lucky to have met Jilly,' she added. 'She has her paw on the pulse of Puddle. Knows everyone!'

It was clear to Gizmo that Lola was itching to keep running. He felt he had to speak quickly before she dashed off again.

'Lola, do you know anyone in the village who might like to adopt one of Jilly's puppies?' he asked her.

'Oh! Moving out, are they? Exciting!' She had a quick think.

'Not off the top of my head, but I'll let you know if anyone comes to mind. Bye!' she added before sprinting off in the direction of the woods.

'Who was that?' asked Wilfred, who was lagging behind his siblings because he'd been distracted by a pigeon. 'She was speedy!'

'That was Lola, Wilfred,'
Jilly told him. 'And yes,
she's always in a hurry.
Why don't we go to the farm now?
Run ahead and tell the others.'

Wilfred did as his mother asked.

'Bunty might know someone,'
Jilly told Gizmo, trying not to
get downhearted.

Gizmo had never been to a
farm before. The route there
took them through a meadow.

As the grass went over Gizmo's head, Jilly suggested she give him a piggyback. The puppies ran ahead, happily exploring the hedgerows. The name of the farm was painted on a sign.

Gizmo read it out loud:

Withy Hook Farm

'I never knew it was called that,' Jilly replied. 'You learn something new every day.'

Bunty was at the farm gate when they arrived. Buzzing round her head was a fly whose name, Bunty told Gizmo, was Fliss.

Being a basset hound, Bunty wasn't that much taller than Gizmo. He decided to dismount to say a proper hello. Unfortunately he landed bottom first in a cowpat! Bunty's fly, Fliss, found this very funny. Bunty snapped at her.

'It happens all the time,' she told Gizmo kindly, and then led him to a water trough. 'Here,' she said, 'you can try and wash off in this.'

While Jilly and Bunty discussed the puppy problem, Gizmo took a deep breath and scrambled up on one end of the trough. Perching himself on the narrow edge, he slowly lowered his backside into the water. Unfortunately, as he

did so, a cow came along for a drink,
and the shock of seeing her made
him fall completely into the water.

The cow kindly grabbed Gizmo by the collar and fished him out, and then proceeded to lick him. This tickled so much it made Gizmo roll around. As he did so, bits of straw from the farmyard stuck to him.

'Maybe you should take him over to the salon,' suggested Bunty, eyeing Gizmo, who was now looking like a scarecrow. 'Bruno could put him under the dryer.'

Gizmo felt a bit of a fool, but Jilly was happy to see her puppies enjoying his antics.

'Sorry I couldn't help,' Bunty said quietly. 'But I'll let you know if I have any ideas.'

Jilly nodded her thanks to Bunty and allowed a soggy Gizmo to climb up on to her back.

Together they headed for
the heart of the village.

The main street of Puddle was
lined with trees and had a few
small shops. The first of these was a
hairdresser. In the doorway lay an
Alsatian called Bruno.

Bruno was very understanding. When his human was busy chatting with her customer, he sneaked Gizmo and Jilly to the back of the salon. Gizmo was beginning to shake from the cold. Jilly helped Gizmo on to a chair and Bruno set up an old-fashioned dryer to warm him up. It didn't take long before Gizmo was feeling much better, if a little fuzzy. He saw Jilly whisper in Bruno's ear

and glance at the puppies. Bruno
looked very serious, but shook
his head.

Gizmo was beginning to feel
he wasn't being much help to Jilly.
He could see she was getting more
and more worried. Even the
puppies seemed to know something
was wrong. Their tails weren't
wagging as much any more.

Their journey home took
them past Puddle train station.

A Jack Russell terrier was busying himself on the platform, but he stopped when he saw Jilly. Jilly introduced Gizmo to Bob, the station dog.

Gizmo waited patiently while Jilly explained the puppy problem to Bob. Bob promised her that he'd mention it to every dog who came through the station.

'Oh dear, can't you read, my friend?' Bob asked Gizmo. Gizmo turned his head to see that the bench he'd been sitting on had a WET PAINT sign.

'The colour suits you,' Jilly teased him as they walked home.

Gizmo laughed. He was amazed how kind she could be even when she was so worried about her puppies. It made him more determined than ever to help her.

'I'm sorry we didn't find anyone to take the puppies, but we shall have to just keep asking,' he reassured her.

'There's not much time left, Gizmo,' replied Jilly sadly.

When they got back home, the
puppies went for a nap and Jilly
and Gizmo decided to draw up
a plan at his house.

It didn't take long before Jilly
was hungry. 'Let's see if Grannie

has anything for us to eat,'
suggested Gizmo, trying to think
of something nice for Jilly.

'Sausages?!' asked Jilly. Her
tail gave a half-hearted wag.

Gizmo wagged his tail too.

On the way to the kitchen,
he showed her Grannie's office,
which had thousands of books.
Grannie had unpacked a lot of
them, but some were still in boxes.

'I've never seen this many books

before,' Jilly remarked in wonder.

'Grannie is the best newspaper editor in the world,' Gizmo told her proudly, sitting down on a comfy pile of packaging.

Jilly gazed at the framed newspaper articles which lined the walls – some of Grannie's finest work.

'Oh,' she said, laughing gently at Gizmo. 'You seem to have sat on something ...'

To The Doghouse by Virginia Woof

The Hundred and One Dalmatians

Mansfield Bark by Jane Pawsten

Following a lead by A. Barker

GILE FR

Gizmo spun round; a piece of packing tape had become attached to his bottom. He could see big letters on it. 'What does it say? What does it say?!' he asked Jilly.

Jilly stopped laughing. 'I must get

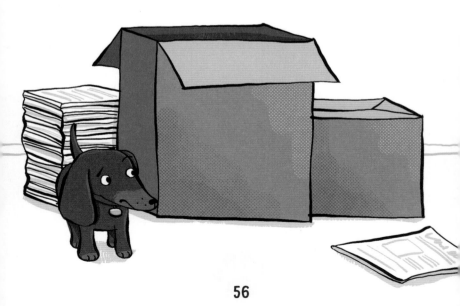

back to the puppies now,' she said.
As she walked out of the open back
door, her head hung low. Gizmo
felt he must have said something
wrong, but he didn't know what.

However, he
didn't have time to
think it through, as
Grannie appeared.

'There you are!' she
said, picking him up.
'Now, why have you got this stuck
on your bottom? You silly sausage!
I can see you need a bath.'

Gizmo snuggled his head next
to Grannie's as she carried him
up the stairs.

During bath time, Gizmo thought about Jilly. He was determined to help her. And as Grannie wrapped him in his favourite towel, a brilliant idea began to form and he couldn't wait to tell Jilly about it.

While Grannie slept, Gizmo crept
downstairs and into her office. He
found a pile of old magazines to sit
on and started typing on Grannie's
old typewriter. It took him all night
to think up words that would catch

his readers' attention. But as the sun rose he was finally finished. He was sure Jilly was going to be pleased.

After gobbling his breakfast in double-quick time, Gizmo rushed next door. Jilly was just supervising the puppies' breakfast when he burst in and dropped a piece of paper on the floor.

'Hold the front page,' he barked. 'I've had an idea!'

Gizmo pushed the piece of paper towards Jilly. 'Ta-da!' he said proudly.

Jilly looked blank. 'What is it?' she asked.

Gizmo was a little confused.

'It's a newspaper bulletin, of course! Look at the headline!'

Gizmo read it out loud.

'Go on,' said Jilly, lying down to listen.

Gizmo cleared his throat.

'Puddle favourite Jilly the Irish wolfhound has a puppy problem. Her four puppies – Wolfie, Wilma, Wilfred and Willabelle – are going to be sent to the four corners of the country unless you can help. Stop this tragedy, lend a paw, and help keep Jilly's puppies within barking distance! Encourage humans with happy homes to come to Pine Tree Close tomorrow. Find the puppies a home!'

'Oh, Gizmo!' cheered Jilly.

'I used some of Grannie's best journalist phrases there, could you tell?'

'It's brilliant!' she said. 'What's the blank bit for?'

'That's why I'm here. I need a photo of the puppies. I've brought Grannie's old Polaroid camera.'

Gizmo had left it outside the cat
flap, so as he went to retrieve it
Jilly explained to the puppies what
was happening. When she was sure
they all understood, she licked
them into shape and they lined
up on the lawn.

'Three ... two ... one ... say fleas!'
Gizmo pressed the button with his
nose and the photo shot out of the
camera. They all gathered round it,
waiting for it to develop.

'Lovely!' exclaimed Gizmo.

'What are you going to do now?' asked Jilly.

'Well, I'll add this picture to the article and then I'll use Grannie's photocopier and print off enough copies for every dog in Puddle. I haven't really thought about

how I'm going to distribute it
yet though ...'

Jilly gave him a big grin. 'Leave
it to me,' she said. 'We can speak
to Chester in the newsagent's.
He can take them on the paper
round. Oh, I could eat you up!'

'Sausage dog, not sausage,
remember, Jilly!' said Gizmo, his
voice a little high-pitched.

'Don't worry, I remember,' Jilly
reassured him.

Gizmo hurried back home to add
the picture to the article. Then,
while Grannie was working in
the garden, he copied it on Grannie's

photocopier. When he signalled
through the window, Jilly came
around to the front door with
something to carry the copies
in. They filled it up and, trying
to look like they weren't doing
anything unusual, headed for
the newsagent's.

An old Scottie dog was standing in the doorway.

'Chester, we need your help!' Jilly barked.

'Oh aye,' said the Scottie dog slowly. 'And what can I do for you?'

'We need you to include this in your paper round,' said Gizmo. 'It's for all the dogs in the village.'

Chester took a look at Gizmo's article and raised his impressive eyebrows.

'Anything for you, Jilly,' he said. 'Leave them there.'

They did as they were told, keeping a few back for the walk home.

'Gizmo,' Jilly said anxiously, 'do you really think this will work?'

'I hope so,' Gizmo replied. 'All we can do now is wait.'

5

Gizmo scrambled through the
fence to Jilly's house early the
next morning. He'd made a sign,
which he dragged after him.

Jilly had already lined the
puppies up on the front porch.

They were under strict instruction
to be on their best behaviour, and
so far it was going OK.

'I made a sign!' Gizmo declared
cheerfully.

'What does it say?' asked Jilly.

'Oh dear, is my writing that bad?' asked Gizmo. He read it aloud.

'It's perfect!' said Jilly, trying to break up a play fight between Wilfred and Willabelle.

Once the puppies had settled, they took to watching the gate hopefully.

'Do you think anyone's going to turn up, Mummy?' asked Wilma.

'I'm sure they will, my darling,' said Jilly, but Gizmo could tell by her voice that she wasn't at all sure.

'I can hear someone,' said Wilfred, who had very good hearing.

And then all of a sudden everyone was there.

First through the gate was Bunty with Val the farmer and her friend Eric.

'Well, if Bunty hadn't run off this morning, we'd never have followed her here, would we, Eric,' Val said. 'Just look at those adorable puppies. You should take one of them home!'

Eric scratched his beard.

'You have heaps of space at your farm,' Val encouraged him. 'And a puppy would be good company. I wouldn't be without Bunty, even if she does sometimes go missing!'

Bunty wagged her tail. Eric crouched down and held out a hand to Wilma. She ignored it and climbed straight into the big pocket of his coat. 'Looks like this one's coming with me!' Eric laughed.

'My dog dragged me here too!' said a tall man who had come from the other side of the village with his young son. 'We were taking Rex here for a walk. We normally just head to the park, but he seemed determined we come this way and here we are. Would you just look at those gorgeous puppies!'

'Can we have one, pleeeease!' pleaded the boy. 'I'll tidy my room for a whole year, please!' The boy

held one of Rex's dog treats
out to Willabelle, who pounced on
it and began to chew. Once she'd
finished she licked the boy's
face – her customary
greeting.

Gizmo made his way over to Jilly. For the first time since he had met her, her long tail was wagging happily. 'I think your plan is working!' she told him.

A family from just the other end of Pine Tree Close were the next to fall in love with a puppy. They chose Wilfred.

'That just leaves Wolfie,' said
Jilly. Gizmo could tell she was
feeling a little nervous for him.
He was the naughty one, after all.

Gizmo searched the crowd, then spotted the perfect owner for Wolfie – a truck driver who lived near Withy Hook Farm. 'Wolfie'll have lots of great adventures if he's adopted by a truck driver. That way he'll get to see the country and he'll still be able to see you and the other puppies.'

'You'd be great company on the road,' said Annabelle, the truck driver, bending down to

talk to Wolfie, who was tugging at
her trouser leg playfully. 'I was just

passing by when I saw the crowd.'
She and Wolfie instantly seemed
to like each other. 'There's plenty
of room in the truck for you,' she
said. Wolfie was
so excited he
had a little
accident,
which made
Annabelle
laugh all the
more. She

bent down and picked him up.

'I can see you're going to be trouble,' she joked. Wolfie smothered her in kisses. He was smitten.

Jilly was so relieved, but Gizmo could see she was also sad to see them go. 'They're all grown up now,' she said to him. 'But they'll always be my babies. I'm so glad I'll still be able to see them. Thank you for helping us.'

When the
humans had gone,
Gizmo was delighted
to be congratulated by
all his new friends.

'You're clearly a natural writer,'
said Jilly.

'You know, I know a bit about sports,' said Lola. 'I could be your sports reporter, if you like.'

'And I could do travel,' said Bob. 'I know the train timetable off by heart.'

'I know a thing or two about beauty,' said Bruno with pride.

'And being a farmer, Bunty should do the weather reports,' suggested Bob.

Bunty wagged her tail.

'Looks like you've got a newspaper on your hands,' said Jilly. 'What are you going to call it?'

Gizmo thought for a moment.

'The **Daily Bark**,' he said.

'That's a good name,' said Jilly.

'And I want you to be my lead reporter,' said Gizmo.

'No, no,' said Jilly. 'Give that job to someone else.'

Gizmo was crestfallen. 'But you know everyone in Puddle. I thought you'd like to, now the puppies have left home.

You do have your paw on the pulse of Puddle,' he added, trying to win her round. 'Why don't you want to do it?'

'I just don't, Gizmo,' said Jilly, and she walked off.

The following morning, Gizmo was
still feeling worried about Jilly. On
his walk into town he bumped into
Lola. She didn't know what the
matter was with Jilly, but she had
some great ideas for an article on

the pros and cons of chasing balls versus frisbees.

Bunty didn't know what the matter was either. 'Has she got a fly?' she asked. 'They can be very troublesome,' she added, snapping at, and missing, Fliss.

'Perhaps she's hungry,' said Bob. 'She does have quite a healthy appetite.'

'Good thinking,' replied Gizmo.

But it was Chester who had the best idea. 'Have you asked her what the matter is?'

Armed with some sausages from
Grannie's kitchen and a card,
Gizmo made his way over to Jilly's.
She was lying in her kennel
looking lonely, but lifted her head

at the scent of the sausages.

'I thought these might cheer
you up!' said Gizmo.

Jilly wagged her tail and tucked in happily.

'And I wrote you this card,' said Gizmo proudly, showing her.

Suddenly Jilly seemed unhappy again. She pushed the card to one side.

'See, I drew a picture of the two of us,' said Gizmo, showing her. 'You're much taller in real life, obviously, but I didn't have enough space on the page.'

'It's a very nice drawing,' said
Jilly.

'The message is even better!'

'Gizmo, you're like a dog with a
bone!' exclaimed Jilly, exasperated.
'I can't read the message.'

'I know, my writing's not very good,' agreed Gizmo.

'It's not your writing,' said Jilly quietly. 'Gizmo, I can't read.'

Gizmo stepped back in shock, accidentally tipping Jilly's water bowl. She moved away and lay on her side.

'You mean you really can't read?' he asked her.

'Yes, Gizmo, I really can't read,' she replied miserably.

Things were beginning to make sense to Gizmo. 'So when you didn't know the name of Bunty's farm, it was because –'

'– I've never been able to read the sign,' sighed Jilly.

'And when I had the FRAGILE label on my bottom, you wouldn't tell me what it said because –'

'– I didn't know,' said Jilly.

'And I remember now, you asked me to read my news article to you. Why didn't you say?'

'I didn't want you to think I was stupid,' replied Jilly.

'I don't think you're stupid,' replied Gizmo. 'That's why it says in your card, "You're the best."

You're the BEST

Because you are, Jilly. You know everyone, and you always know what to do. You never get anything stuck on your bottom or fall into water troughs, and you introduced me to all your friends.'

'But I can't read,' said Jilly.

'You can learn to, if you like,' said Gizmo.

Jilly thought for a while. 'Well, now that the puppies have left home, I will have more time ...' she said slowly.

'I'm sure there's someone in the village who could teach you,' Gizmo encouraged her.

Suddenly Jilly wagged her tail. 'Actually, Gizmo, I know just the right dog,' she said.

'You always know the right dog,' replied Gizmo. 'Who is it?'

'You!' she barked.

They started the very next day. Jilly turned out to be an excellent student. She and Gizmo went through letters and words in the morning, and by lunchtime she could read the word 'SAUSAGE'.

In the afternoon she and the rest of the gang told Gizmo all their ideas for stories. And he, as editor-in-chief, decided which would make it into the very first edition of the Daily Bark.

'Bertie the Labrador gave me this,' said Jilly, handing it to Gizmo. 'I think it's a recipe. Can we include it?'

'Does horse manure really count as a recipe?' asked Gizmo, reading quickly. He was busy cutting up words and working out what the front-page headline should be.

'I think it does to Bertie,' replied Jilly.

'There, now what do you think of this?' asked Gizmo, unveiling the headline to everyone.

Jilly looked at it carefully. 'I'm sure it's good,' she said. 'But I think we've got a better one.' The dogs of the Daily Bark unfurled a piece of paper to reveal a headline made from cut-out letters.

NEW DOG IN TOWN SAVES PUPS!

Gizmo didn't know whether to bark or wag. In the end he turned in a circle twice and sat down.

'I hope you don't mind, but I got the others to help with the article too,' Jilly said.

Bunty, Bob, Lola and Bruno
cheered Gizmo and they all helped
to stick together the front page
and make copies
for every dog
in Puddle.

As they walked down to see
Chester at the newsagent's, Gizmo
had never felt so happy.

Watch out for more

NEWS HOUNDS

stories

COMING SOON!

Read all Fabio's adventures

Available now

About the Author and Illustrator

LAURA JAMES has two writing companions, her wire-haired dachshunds, Brian and Florence. They are a constant source of inspiration for her stories and she adores their every bark, tail-wag, and tummy-rub request. Sometimes she wonders if they might secretly be writing about her too!

CHARLIE ALDER lives in Devon, England, with her husband and son. When not drawing chickens or dogs, Charlie can be found in her studio drinking coffee, arranging her crayons and inventing more accidental animal heroes.